ONLY A
WITCH CAN FLY

by Alison McGhee   illustrated by Taeeun Yoo

Feiwel and Friends   New York, NY

To Laurel McGhee Blackett, with love and admiration —A. M.

To Jungeun, Youngeun and Taehyun...with love —T. Y.

This book is written as a sestina, a very old form of poetry that originated with French troubadours in the 12th century. It consists of six six-line stanzas followed by a three-line stanza. The same words, or related words, end the lines of each of the six-line stanzas, but in a different order each time. The same six words appear in the final three-line stanza, as well.

A FEIWEL AND FRIENDS BOOK • An Imprint of Macmillan

LIBRARY OF CONGRESS CATALOGING-IN-PUBLICATION DATA • McGhee, Alison. Only a witch can fly : a picture book / by Alison McGhee ; illustrated by Taeeun Yoo. — 1st ed. p. cm. Summary: A young girl wants to fly like a witch on a broom, and one special night, through enormous effort and with the help of her brother, her black cat, and an owl, she fulfills her dream. ISBN-13: 978-0-312-37503-4 / ISBN-10: 0-312-37503-4 [1. Stories in rhyme. 2. Witches—Fiction. 3. Growth—Fiction. 4. Flight—Fiction.] I. Yoo, Taeeun, ill. II. Title. PZ8.3.M45956Onl 2009 [E]—dc22 2008028542

First Edition: August 2009   10 9 8 7 6 5 4 3 2 1

Feiwel and Friends logo designed by Filomena Tuosto

Book design by Rich Deas

www.feiwelandfriends.com

If you were a young witch, who had not yet flown,
and the dark night sky held a round yellow moon

and the moon shone light on the silent broom
and the dark Cat beside you purred, *Soar*,
would you too, begin to cry,
because of your longing to fly?

The dark night around you fills with *Fly, fly*
and bright yellow moonlight shines down.
Cat, by your side, purrs a gentle *Bye, bye*
and Owl stares up at a star, so far.

**Your heart tells you *now* and you walk to the door.
Cat arches his back and croons, *Soon*.**

You stroke dear Cat and slip from your home,
your home in the woods by the fire,
cauldron and hat, brown velvet Bat,
the too-small robe you once wore.

Far above are the stars you love,
singing their faraway tune,

but black Cat beside you hums,
Poor you, poor, poor.

How awful it is not to fly in the sky

with the moon and the stars so high
and the smoke rising up like a plume.
Black Cat beside you cries, *Look at the star*,
and brown velvet Bat's echoes sigh.

You pick up the broom and you turn to the moon
and you count,

One,

Two,

Three,

Four —

and into the sky you soar.

Black Cat arches and sings, *Higher, high*
and the dark hearth below is gone.
Above you the night birds circle and croon.
Did you ever know you could fly so high?
The top of the sky is so far. So far.

The moon trails fire through a reservoir,
and you are earthbound no more.
Who could have known it was such a big sky?
Bat and Owl below wave *Bye, bye*
and Cat calls a velvet song to the moon.
And you? You have flown . . .

you have flown!

Hold tight to your broom
and float past the stars,
and turn to the heavens and soar.
For only a witch can fly past the moon.

Only a witch can fly.